THE FUNNY OLD MAN
AND
THE FUNNY OLD WOMAN

by Martha Barber
Illustrated by Gillian Campbell

MONDO

This edition first published in the United States of America in 1996
by **MONDO Publishing**

By arrangement with MULTIMEDIA INTERNATIONAL (UK) LTD

For information contact:
MONDO Publishing
980 Avenue of the Americas
New York, NY 10018

Printed in Hong Kong
First Mondo printing, July 1996
01 02 03 04   9 8 7 6 5

Originally published in Australia in 1987 by Horwitz Publications Pty Ltd
Original development by Robert Andersen & Associates and Snowball Educational
Cover redesign by Michael Mendelsohn

Library of Congress Cataloging-in-Publication Data
Barber, Martha.
    Funny old man and funny old woman / by Martha Barber ;
illustrated by Gillian Campbell.
        p.   cm.
    Summary: Thinking that their cow is sick, a funny old man
and a funny old woman make a variety of adjustments to get her to
the doctor.
        ISBN 1-57255-173-9 (pbk. : alk. paper). — ISBN 1-57255-174-7
(big book pbk. : alk. paper)
        [1. Cows—Fiction 2. Stories in rhyme.] I. Campbell, Gillian, ill.
II. Title.
PZ8.3.B235Fu   1996
{Fic]—dc20   95-49116
                                                                  CIP
                                                                   AC

A funny old man and a funny old woman
sat by the fire one night.
"Funny old man," the old woman said,
"I don't know what to do.
When I went to the barn to milk the cow,
the funny old cow wouldn't moo."

The funny old man scratched his head.
"I know what to do," he said.
"Take her to town to see Doctor Brown,
and bring her home in the morning.
That's what you do when your cow won't
    moo."

"But she's out in the woodshed lying down.
How will you take the cow to town
and bring her back in the morning?"

"If she can't walk," said the funny old man,
"I'll push her in the wheelbarrow if I can,
and walk her home in the morning."

"But the goat's asleep in the wheelbarrow.
Where shall I put the goat?"

"Put the goat on top of the garden gate.
The goat can sleep there very late
till the cow comes home in the morning."

"But the rooster is roosting on the garden
    gate.
Where shall I put the rooster?"

"Put the rooster in the butter churn,
so tight that he can't twist or turn
till the cow comes home in the morning."

"But my nice fresh butter is in the churn.
Where shall I put the butter?"

"Put the butter on a string in the garden
        pool
and it will keep there fresh
        and cool
till the cow comes home
        in the morning."

"But the fish is in the garden pool.
Where shall I put the fish?"

"Put the fish in some water in the old
        washtub,
so he can give his fins a scrub
till the cow comes home in the morning."

"But the cat's asleep in the old washtub.
Where shall I put the cat?"

"Put the cat in the fruit bowl. Then she'll
      dream
of nice red strawberries laced with cream
till the cow comes home in the morning."

"But the figs are in the fruit bowl.
Where shall I put the figs?"

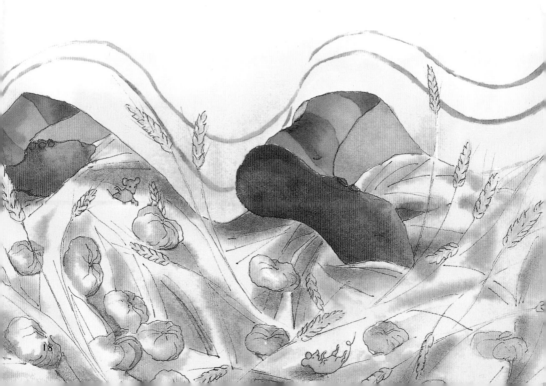

"Put the figs in the barn on a pile of wheat.
They'll keep quite firm and fresh and sweet
till the cow comes home in the morning."

"But the pig is sleeping on the pile of
wheat.
What shall I do with the pig?"

"Put the pig on a pillow in the feather bed,
to snooze and snore," the old man said,
"till the cow comes home in the morning."

"No," said the woman. "I sleep on the bed.
Where shall I lay my funny old head?"

The old man cried, "Put the pig in the bed!
And you can stand on your funny old head
till the cow comes home in the morning."

So the funny old woman flipped up on her
   head.
"It's really quite cozy here," she said,
"till the cow comes home in the morning."

Then late that night the funny old man
pushed the funny old cow to town.

They rolled in the light of the bright, full
moon
till they found old Doctor Brown.

The doctor thumped on the old cow's
    hide,
he tickled her tonsils and looked inside.
"Old man," said the doctor, "your cow's
    not sick.
She merely wanted the ride!"

The old man cried, "Can this be true?"
The cow replied with a happy *moo*.

And they both went home in the morning.